Disney

Hundred-Acre Adventures

Sticky Paws

Ladybird

Winnie the Pooh is truly a 'Bear-Of-Very-Little-Brain', but he knows how to think hard sometimes. One morning he woke up humming a song he had invented.

'If night is dark,

it's because it doesn't wash!

But when day breaks

the sun will wash it clean!

And if Pooh washes too

he will shine as bright as the sun!'

Winnie the Pooh frowned. He was a very confused bear.

'Hmm, do I need to wash because I'm dirty?'

The first thing Pooh usually thought about in the morning was honey, but that day he was worried about washing and not his rumbly tumbly!

'No time to waste! Exercise first! I'll think about washing later!' announced Pooh to no-one in particular.

Pooh did his exercises very quickly that morning, he touched his toes, bent his knees and pulled his tummy in. But when he had finished, he was still confused. Pooh needed to think.

'Am I dirty now?' he wondered.

Pooh went to the pond and sat on a rock in the middle of the water. He began to wash himself. The honey soap smelled so good he could have licked it!

Soon Pooh's mind turned from getting clean, to getting full. His tummy rumbled and he knew it was time to eat, and eat, and eat. Along with lunch and tea and dinner, breakfast was Pooh's favourite meal. He hurried home as fast as his legs could take him.

'Dear honey pots, I wish you a day full of greedy bears!' laughed Pooh as he emptied his first pot of honey. Several drops fell on his clean fur, it made it shiny but terribly sticky again.

'To the pond to wash!' cried Pooh. 'Then some more breakfast!'

Winnie the Pooh made several trips to the pond to clean off the sticky, golden honey. He would have spent the whole day doing this but, being a greedy little bear, he soon ran out of honey.

'Oh, bother!' said Pooh. 'And I'm still hungry!'

When evening came, Pooh was very tired because he had spent the whole day searching for new honey trees. He went to Kanga's, covered in honey, a little dirt and several bee stings.

'Dear, oh dear! I think you need to hop in the bath with Roo!' said Kanga.

'What bath?' cried Roo. 'Pooh's dirty, not me!'

'My darling,' Kanga replied, 'there's the dirt you can see and the dirt you can't see.'

'Oh look, here comes Piglet!' cried Roo. 'I am sure he remembers the day you gave him a bath and then no one recognised him!'

'That just proves how clean Piglet had become!' Kanga replied. 'He just didn't know how dirty he was before!'

Piglet looked frightened.

'I don't want another bath! It will make me all fluffy and I will lose my colours!' yelled Piglet as he ran away from Kanga and Pooh.

Roo didn't want a bath either, he silently crept out after Piglet.

'Why don't they like being clean?' Kanga wondered. 'I don't understand.'

'Neither do I,' Pooh replied. 'I suppose they forgot you always get a snack after getting clean.'

'What about you, Pooh? Don't you like feeling clean, smelling good and having your fur soft and shiny?' asked Kanga, smiling.

'Well, I, erm... suppose so. Christopher Robin told me you should always wash your hands before eating. And I, have just washed my hands,' said Pooh with a cheeky grin.

Kanga held out the cookie jar for Pooh.

'Here's your cookie, you greedy bear!' laughed Kanga. 'Now, listen to me, we are going to play a little joke on our other sticky pawed friends.'

Kanga sent Pooh over to Tigger's house.

'Who is it? It isn't Kanga is it?' asked a nervous Tigger.

'Open up Tigger, it's me, Pooh!' replied Pooh.

Pooh walked in to find all his friends huddled together in a corner, shaking with fear.

'My friends here do not want a bath, and neither do I!' Owl declared.

'There is no point washing,' grumbled Rabbit, 'since you always get dirty again! It is simply a waste of time!'

'I washed my ears last month,' explained Eyeore. 'Why wear them out by washing them too much?'

'Too much soap, and off go my stripes!' added Tigger for good measure.

16

'I have good news for you,' Pooh announced. 'Kanga has invited us all for an afternoon snack!'

'Does she expect us to wash?' Rabbit asked suspiciously.

'Not at all!' Pooh replied, smiling.

'Do you mean that even I don't have to wash?' Roo asked.

'Even you! Your mum says she cannot force anyone to wash,' said Pooh.

When the friends reached Kanga's house, they saw that it had changed quite a lot. There were spots all over the tablecloth, dirty dishes piled up in the sink and there were lots of greasy papers all over the kitchen floor.

'May I have a clean bowl, please?' asked Roo, nervously.

Kanga opened her eyes very wide.

'But Roo, what is the use of washing them since you will make them dirty eventually when you eat? Tell me, may I wipe my hands on you?' Kanga asked as she raised her chocolate covered hands towards Roo.

'**N**o!' cried Roo. 'You are too dirty!'

'All right, then I suppose I should go and wash them,' said Kanga.

The friends had an idea.

When Kanga returned, she was as clean and beautiful as ever. And to her surprise the kitchen had been entirely cleaned up!

'Mum, I feel dirty,' said Roo sheepishly. 'It itches a little and I feel really sticky.'

'Would you like to have a bath?' Kanga asked.

Roo smiled.

'Oh! yes, please, right away!'

Since a bath is never as pleasant as when there are many of your friends in the tub, everyone jumped in. There were lots of bubbles and splashing as the friends got clean.

Kanga washed the tablecloth and put it on the line to dry.

'Should we dry on the line, too?' Roo asked.

'Don't be silly. I'll get you some clean, dry clothes,' replied Kanga. 'And tomorrow, who knows, maybe you will all have fun getting dirty again!'